BUNNY TROUBLE

ISBN 0-590-33601-0

Copyright © 1985 by Hans Wilhelm Inc.

12 11 10 9 8 7   7 8 9/8 0/9

Printed in the U.S.A.   08

SCHOLASTIC INC.
New York Toronto London Auckland Sydney Tokyo

BUNNY
TROUBLE

by HANS WILHELM

Once there was a rabbit colony that was different from any other. The rabbits here were in charge of decorating all the Easter eggs for the Easter Bunny to deliver.

Everyone worked year 'round getting ready.

Everyone except Ralph. He cared for only one thing in the world—soccer.

It worried his mother and father.

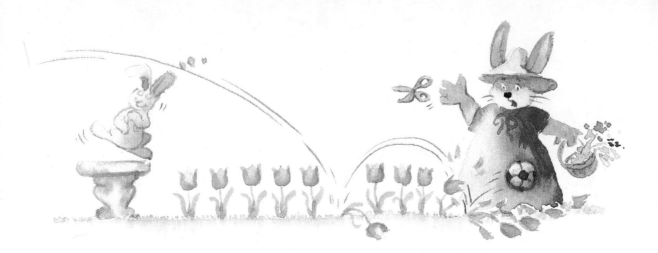

It worried the other rabbits in the colony.

It worried his teachers in the school where all the young rabbits went to learn egg decorating. Where was Ralph while everyone else was hard at work in the classroom? He was outside working on his fancy footwork.

It worried his sister Liza—especially when he ruined her birthday party.

Liza loved Ralph more than anyone else in the world. But she knew that one day he would get into trouble. He just didn't fit in.

Each year as Easter
approached, everyone got
busier and busier. The chickens
laid more eggs. The painters,
the jelly bean makers, and the
basket stuffers all worked
overtime.

Ralph had to work, too. But he had a hard time keeping his mind on his job.

Instead, he was thinking about place kicks, and he tried just one. Oooops! Over went a full basket of eggs.

The exhausted chickens groaned. The rabbits shouted at Ralph. "Go play soccer on the other side of the trees so we can finish our work in peace," they said.

Ralph was glad to go. He went off to play by himself on the other side of the forest.

That night, he did not come home.

His mother wept and wrung her hands. "Where could he be?"
she wondered. "And with Easter just two days away."

Morning came. Still Ralph had not come home. Liza slipped out to search for him.

She found him not far away — locked up in a cage.

A farmer had caught him while he was practicing his dribble in the cauliflower field.

"The coach always told us to look where we were going, not at our feet," Ralph joked sorrowfully.

"Don't worry," Liza told him. "I'll go and get help."

She ran back, past the busy rabbits, calling, "Mama, mama, we must save Ralph. The farmer has caught him and is going to make him into Easter dinner!"

"Oh, I knew that bunny would get into trouble someday," wept mama as she followed Liza to Ralph's cage.

It had thick bars and a heavy padlock.

"We'll never get him out of there," moaned their mother when she saw Ralph inside.

"Of course we will," said Liza firmly. "I think I can get the lock open."

Liza worked for hours. But the lock refused to be picked. The bars wouldn't bend. The door couldn't be pried off.

"If I ever get free," whispered Ralph, "I promise I will never play soccer again."

"No, Ralph," said Liza, "you want to be a soccer player. And you will be, too. But you also have to help with the eggs."

"And not be such a nuisance," added mama.

Ralph knew they were right. He promised to do what they said.

Hours passed. Suddenly Liza cried, "I've got an idea that will do the trick! But we have to hurry."

Liza and mama ran all the way home. In no time, Liza was back carrying a small bundle under her arms. She squeezed it carefully through the bars of Ralph's cage. Then she whispered the plan.

The next morning there was a
great commotion around the cage.

Inside it, next to Ralph, was a basket of the most beautiful Easter eggs anyone had ever seen. Some were polka-dotted, some were dyed deep purple, and some were painted with rainbows.

The farmer's children gathered around. "He must be the Easter Bunny," they exclaimed with wonder. "How else could he have gotten those eggs? We must let him go or there won't be any Easter for us."

So the farmer opened the cage door.

Ralph ran home as fast as he could.

But he didn't forget Liza's words. He did try harder with his painting.

Ralph even became known for one special design, which he did far better than anyone else, and almost as well as kicking, passing, and scoring.